22 DEC 2010

I0635348

XMAS

This book should be returned/renewed by
the latest date shown above. Overdue items
incur charges which prevent self-service
renewals. Please contact the library.

Wandsworth Libraries
24 hour Renewal Hotline
01159 293388
www.wandsworth.gov.uk

THE BRIGHTER BOROUGH

Wandsworth

L.749A (2.07)

500 412 262 D5

If you enjoy Christmas Quackers you should try these other great Young Hippo stories by Sylvia Green:

The Soft-Hearted Sheepdog
A Parsnip Called Val

"Action packed and funny. We'd like to read more books by Sylvia Green."

Laburnum class, Barnwood School, Guildford

And here are even more wonderful animal stories from Young Hippo!

Ripper and Fang
Margaret Clarke

Hands Off Our Hens!
Jennifer Curry

Esther and the Baby Baboon
Susan Gates

Big Puss, Little Mouse
Kara May

Guinea Pig's Adventure
Pat Posner

SYLVIA GREEN

Christmas
Quackers

Illustrated by Annabel Spenceley

For Charlie

500 412262

Scholastic Children's Books,
Commonwealth House, 1-19 New Oxford Street,
London WC1A 1NU, UK
a division of Scholastic Ltd
London ~ New York ~ Toronto ~ Sydney ~ Auckland
Mexico City ~ New Delhi ~ Hong Kong

Published in the UK by Scholastic Ltd, 1999

Text copyright © Sylvia Green, 1999
Illustrations copyright © Annabel Spenceley, 1999

ISBN 0 439 01177 9

Printed by Cox & Wyman Ltd, Reading, Berks.

1 2 3 4 5 6 7 8 9 10

Chapter 1

The Science Project

How could anyone concentrate on maths when something so exciting was about to happen?

Kate chewed thoughtfully on the end of her long pigtail and stared at the egg in the heated tank next to her desk. It could hatch out any day now.

She blinked. Did it move? Or did she imagine it?

"I think it moved," she whispered to Peter, sitting next to her.

"Shhh," warned Sophie from across the table.

Miss Hancock, their teacher, had brought in the Mallard duck egg for the class to hatch out as part of their science lessons. She helped out at a wildfowl rescue centre in her spare time and the egg had come from a late nest that had been deserted. Apparently the late summer this year had fooled some ducks into laying another clutch of eggs.

Kate stared hard at the precious egg. It had been a lovely surprise when they had come back to school after the summer holidays. For the last three days they had turned the egg and sprinkled it with lukewarm water. And they had put up pictures of the different stages of a duckling's development inside an egg. She couldn't wait to see the real thing.

Then she heard it! A tiny high-pitched cheep!

Kate leapt to her feet. "It cheeped, Miss Hancock. It cheeped. I just heard it. It really did."

The other children jumped up and rushed to crowd round the tank.

Kate was pushed and jostled as all the children tried to see but she stood firm. Being short, she wanted to stay at the front. She wasn't going to miss this.

Miss Hancock joined them. "All right, children. Now keep very quiet and very still. And watch."

"Cheep." The egg moved again and a tiny crack appeared in it. There was a general gasp as the crack got bigger.

"Wow, is that a beak?"

"I think it's a claw."

The shell broke in half and the little duckling wriggled and pushed until its head was free. It blinked in the light.

"Look at its little eyes," whispered Kate. "He can't get his bottom out," giggled Peter.

Another couple of wriggles, a twist and a push, and a perfectly formed duckling covered in wet brown-and-yellow down unfolded itself and lay on the straw.

"Look at its tiny webbed feet."

"Why's it just lying there?" asked Kate.

"It's exhausted," said Miss Hancock. "It took a lot of effort to get out of that egg."

Kate stared at it. She had never seen anything so tiny, so perfect. Peter was standing on her foot but she hardly felt it at all.

The bell went for lunchtime. "I don't want any lunch today, Miss," said Kate. "So I'll just stay here and watch the duckling."

"Don't be silly, Kate," said her teacher. "You must have something to eat. Now run along – the duck will still be here when you get back. It just needs to rest for a while."

Kate crept back into the classroom having swallowed her lunch in record time. She rushed over to the tank. The duckling was on its feet and its fluffy brown-and-yellow down was now quite dry. It was wide awake and looking perky.

"Hello, little duckling," she whispered, crouching down so she was level with him.

"Cheep, cheep," said the duckling.

It took a little jump towards Kate and studied her with bright black eyes. "Cheep, cheep."

"You are so beautiful," said Kate. She felt a lump in her throat. She wasn't sure if it was the emotion of seeing this beautiful little creature or if it was indigestion because she had eaten her lunch too quickly.

"Cheep, cheep."

The door opened and Peter and Sophie came in. "You're not supposed to be in here until after the bell," said Sophie.

Kate didn't take her eyes off the duckling. "I know, but look at him. Isn't he the most beautiful little thing you ever saw?"

"He's cute," said Peter, crouching down beside her.

"He's all right," said Sophie. "But I've been looking for you. I wanted to show you a new dance step I learnt last night."

The bell went then and the rest of the class crowded in, followed by Miss Hancock. They all came to look at the duckling.

"Let's call him Squeak," said Adrian.

"He doesn't squeak, he cheeps," said Emma.

"And he won't always cheep," said Miss Hancock. "As he gets older he'll quack."

"I know. I know what we can call him," said Peter. "Let's call him Quackers."

Kate grinned at him. "Brilliant."

Everyone else agreed.

"Cheep, cheep," said Quackers.

Their teacher carefully lifted him on to a pair of old kitchen scales. The tiny duckling waddled about so much that the needle wouldn't stay still. Eventually Emma was able to enter thirty-five grams on the record chart they had already made.

Miss Hancock put him back in his tank and explained that as well as food he would need water to drink and to bathe his head in.

Kate looked at Quackers.

Quackers looked back at her and cocked his little head on one side. "Cheep, cheep."

She couldn't wait to start looking after him, to watch him grow up.

"Is it a boy or a girl?" asked Adrian.

"It's very difficult to tell at this age," said Miss Hancock. She explained that even when ducklings get their first feathers they all look like females but then towards the end of the year the males develop their beautiful green heads and silver-grey backs. "It's a shame we won't see this one change if it's a boy," she added.

"Why?" asked Kate.

"We're only keeping him for four weeks," said the teacher. "It wouldn't be fair to keep him cooped up here any longer. He's going back to the Wildfowl Rescue Centre. There, he can have some freedom, as well as be looked after until he's old enough to fly away and find himself a pond or a river somewhere."

"Only four weeks?" cried Kate. "But he could live in my garden. I'd look after him. We've got a pond – and Dad can build him a hut."

Kate's father was the school caretaker and they lived next to the school.

"Oh, I don't know," said Miss Hancock. "Although it would be wonderful if we could observe him for longer."

"Please," said Kate.

The other children joined in in agreement. They all wanted to watch Quackers grow up.

"Well, we'll see what your father – and your mother – say," said Miss Hancock.

Kate smiled at Quackers and chewed on the end of her long pigtail thoughtfully. She was already planning what she was going to say to her parents to persuade them to let her keep the little duck. Dad would probably be okay but Mum was definitely more tricky.

Chapter 2

The Audition

Kate smiled to herself as she lifted Quackers on to the scales in the school playground. In the background she could hear her father banging nails into the little duck's new hut in their garden. Good old Dad, she thought. Mum had taken a bit more convincing but she had finally agreed.

Quackers jumped out of the scales again and Kate laughed as she put him back in. "Keep still – just for a moment."

Miss Hancock looked at the dial. "Two hundred and ninety grams," she read. "See how quickly baby ducklings grow."

Peter entered it on Quacker's record chart against his age – three weeks.

Kate had really enjoyed helping to look after Quackers over the past weeks. He had a special rolled-oats mix several times a day and they'd chopped up hard-boiled eggs, nettles and greens. They'd kept his tank clean and recorded his progress on the chart. Today they had noted that his tail and wing feathers were just beginning to grow out of his baby down.

Kate put him gently on to the grass of the school playing fields. They liked him to have an outing every day. She ran off a little way and he immediately followed at her heels. When she stopped, he stopped.

It made everyone laugh the way Quackers followed Kate everywhere.

Miss Hancock had told them that when ducklings first hatch their instinct is to follow the first thing they see. Usually their mother – but in this case – Kate.

"He really thinks you're his mother," Emma laughed.

"Cheep, cheep." Quackers ran after Kate again holding out his tiny stumpy wings.

"Does he think he's a human?" asked Adrian.

"I don't know what he thinks," said Miss Hancock. "But he's never seen another duck so he probably thinks he's one of us – whatever we are."

Quackers started to nibble at the grass. "Oh look. That's the first time he's picked his own grass."

Miss Hancock laughed as he went on to nibble Kate's shoelaces. "He's growing into quite a little character, isn't he? You'd better bring him in though," she said. "Marcus Monday will probably have arrived by now."

The class was putting on a pantomime for Christmas. Marcus Monday, a friend of Miss Hancock and a professional actor, was going to direct it. It was to be performed for the rest of the school and the parents to raise money for the Wildfowl Rescue Centre.

Sophie's eyes lit up. "I can't wait to meet Marcus Monday."

"Is he famous?" asked Emma.

"Course he is," said Sophie. She started walking towards the school building.

Kate joined her, Quackers following

at her heels. "D'you know him then?" She had to look up to her friend who was several inches taller than her.

"Well, no," Sophie admitted. "But he must be famous – he's an actor."

"I've never heard of him," said Peter. "He's never been on the telly."

"Snow White and the Seven Dwarfs is ever such a good pantomime," said Sophie, pushing her long dark curls from her face. "I'm hoping to get the part of Snow White."

"So am I," said Kate. She could just imagine herself up there on the stage in her lovely Snow White costume singing and acting to help little creatures like Quackers at the Wildfowl Rescue Centre. It gave her a warm glow.

Quackers followed Kate into the classroom where all the chairs and tables had been pushed to the sides. Over by the window was a tall thin young man looking through some papers. His hair was long and curly and didn't look as though it would be possible to comb. He looked up at them and dropped the papers down on to a table.

Then, flinging his long thin arms out wide, he strode over to greet them.

"Welcome, welcome," he cried in a loud, deep voice. It seemed much too deep for someone so thin. "Do come in. Gather round."

The children all shuffled forward. They were all used to looking out for Quackers and made a space for him and Kate to get through.

"I'm Marcus Monday and as I expect you've been told I am a member of the theatrical profession."

"I think he means he's an actor," whispered Peter.

"Shh," said Sophie.

Kate went to pick Quackers up to put him back in his tank.

Marcus spotted him. "I say, what have we here?" He gave an exaggerated laugh and bent down to him. "I'm sorry, darling, but we're not doing Mother Goose."

Sophie laughed embarrassingly loudly. "Oh, Marcus, you are funny."

Kate was indignant. She picked Quackers up and faced Marcus. "He's a duck – not a goose."

Marcus peered at Quackers, his long pointed nose almost touching the little duck. "Yes, well, whatever he is, darling, he'll have to go. Artists can't be expected to work with distractions."

All of a sudden Quackers reached up and nipped him on the nose.

"Ouch!" Marcus jumped back holding his nose. He glared at Kate. "That – that creature's dangerous."

Everyone was trying not to laugh – except Sophie who looked horrified.

Miss Hancock rushed to Marcus's side. As Kate took Quackers away she could hear her uttering comforting words to the startled actor.

"What a fuss," Kate whispered to the little duck as she put him in his tank. "You can't possibly have hurt him. You're only tiny."

Marcus quickly regained control and as Kate joined the others he began reading out a list of the different parts in the pantomime. He wanted them all to choose a part they would like to play. Then he would get them to read a bit from the script and see if they were suitable. An audition, he said it was.

"Now, all those who would like to play Snow White come over here to me," he said.

Sophie was there first – which wasn't difficult as she hadn't left Marcus's side since they came in. Kate joined her and two other girls.

Marcus looked over the four hopeful girls in front of him. His eyes rested on Kate and he put his hand to his nose for a second. "Not you, darling. You're too short. Why don't you audition for one of the dwarfs?"

"A dwarf?" Kate stamped off, furious. She went and sat on the table next to Quackers's tank chewing vigorously on her pigtail. The little duck came over to her and pecked on the glass. "Cheek," she whispered to him. "I'm not a bit like a dwarf."

Sophie had now pulled herself up to her full height and was fluttering her eyelashes at Marcus. "I can dance – and sing," she told him. "And I want to be an actress when I grow up."

Peter came to sit with Kate as the three remaining girls all read from the script.

Sophie got the part. The others didn't really stand a chance beside her.

Marcus seemed pleased with her. "It's a big part, darling," he told her. "You might need a bit of extra coaching from me to learn all the songs. Do you think you can manage that?"

"Just try and stop her," Peter whispered as Sophie nodded eagerly.

Joshua was chosen as the handsome prince and Cathy as the wicked queen. Peter got the part of the man in the mirror as he had a good strong voice. Now Marcus was asking for children who wanted to audition for the seven dwarfs.

Kate sat with her arms folded. She didn't want to be a dwarf. She wasn't sure she even wanted to be in the pantomime now.

"Go on," said Peter. "It is to help the Wildfowl Rescue Centre."

Kate thought about it. She looked at Quackers.

"Cheep, cheep," said Quackers.

"All right." Kate got the part of the seventh dwarf – Dopey. Marcus said it was because she was the smallest but she suspected he had done it on purpose.

Kate sat with Quackers as the villagers and foresters were chosen. The little duckling seemed to find it all very exciting and ran up and down in his tank. Every time he cheeped Marcus paused and closed his eyes. Then he took a deep breath and carried on.

Adrian was chosen as the huntsman. The few remaining children would be needed to shift scenery, pull the curtains and prompt.

Marcus had written a part into it for himself. He said it was a tradition going back to the early nineteenth century to have a dame (a man playing the part of a woman – usually a comedy role). He would be Clara the Cook who looks after Snow White when she is banished to the palace kitchens by the wicked queen.

Emma asked him if he was acting in anything at the moment.

"No. I'm resting, darling. Resting."

"I think that means he's out of work," whispered Peter.

"Why does he call everyone 'darling'?" asked Kate.

"It's because he's an actor," said Sophie.

"Do they all talk like that then?"

"Well, some of them."

"He's a bit over the top, isn't he?" said Peter.

They were all given their parts to learn and then Miss Hancock went to see Marcus out. He paused by the door and looked over at Quackers. He touched his nose briefly as he said: "I trust we won't be rehearsing in here. I sincerely hope it will be somewhere more civilized." Then he swept out.

Quackers watched him leave. "Cheep, cheep."

Sophie's eyes were shining. "Isn't Marcus wonderful!"

"Huh, that's a matter of opinion," said Kate.

"Don't be such a misery," said Sophie. "You got a part, didn't you?"

"And it's quite an important part," said Peter. "Being one of the seven dwarfs is almost as important as playing Snow White."

"Well, I wouldn't go that far," said Sophie.

Chapter 3

How Could a Little Duck
Cause Any Trouble?

Kate let Quackers out of the new hut in her garden. He ran out announcing his arrival in a series of excited cheeps.

"Welcome to your new home," said Kate. "Although you haven't actually moved far – just next door. There's the school, over there."

Quackers blinked in the sunlight and then started to nibble the grass.

The little duck's hut had plenty of warm straw and Dad had fixed up an infra-red lamp to keep him warm until all his feathers grew. At four weeks old now his new brown-flecked wing feathers were developing well. A few white feathers were appearing under his rapidly growing tail.

"It's Saturday," Kate told him. "So I'll be home with you for the whole weekend." Their garden was small and enclosed with fences so he would be quite safe. He was only to be shut up at night to keep him warm, and safe from foxes. Miss Hancock had said he was a wild creature and must have the freedom to fly away when he was ready.

Kate looked down at the little duck who had come to sit on her right foot. He didn't look very wild to her. She hoped he would stay for ever.

Dad came out with her little brother Edward. "Hello, young fellow-me-lad," he said to Quackers.

Edward toddled forward. "Naughty duck," he said.

"No he's not," laughed Kate. Then she turned to her father. "Thanks for helping to persuade Mum."

"That's all right," he smiled. "Like I said to her – how could a little duck cause any trouble?"

Her mother came out then and watched the new arrival pecking at a dandelion. "What about Morgan?" she asked.

At the sound of his name the tabby cat

that lived next door appeared over the fence. Kate tensed, ready to rush in and rescue Quackers. She'd forgotten about Morgan.

Morgan looked at Quackers.

Quackers eyed Morgan.

The indignant cat hissed at the intruder.

Then to everyone's surprise it was Quackers who gave chase. He ran after the cat flapping his tiny wings. "Cheep, cheep. Cheep, cheep." The little creature was fearless.

Morgan, who usually considered Kate's family's garden to be his own territory, took one look and fled back over the fence.

He wasn't at all sure about this new arrival.

Dad laughed. "I don't think we need to worry about him."

"Naughty duck," said Edward.

Mum gave a big sigh, rolled her eyes to the top of her head and went back to the house with Edward, tut-tutting.

Kate went to get Quackers's breakfast of moistened grains mixed with soaked bread and vegetables.

Peter and Sophie arrived and Quackers ran to greet them. Peter had brought an apple to cut up for him – the little duck's favourite fruit.

Kate put his bowl of food down and Quackers immediately took a large beakfull. Then he plunged it into his bowl of water, gargling through it.

"Yuck," said Sophie.

Quackers took that as encouragement and advanced towards her.

"Get him away from me," she cried, backing off and holding her skirt out of his reach. "Just look at his mucky beak."

"For heaven's sake, Sophie," said Kate. "Don't be such a pain."

"Well, you spend all your time with him now," she complained, pushing her long dark curls from her face. "It's only a duck. And it's messy – and smelly."

Kate stuffed her hands into her jeans pockets. "He's not."

"Anyway I've brought this for us to watch." Sophie held up a video. "It's Snow White and the Seven Dwarfs."

"Brilliant," said Peter.

"Well..." Kate looked down at Quackers who had gone back to his breakfast. She didn't really want to leave him.

"Come on," said Sophie.

"All right." Kate bent down to Quackers. "You stay here and finish your breakfast. And then I promise I'll spend the rest of the day with you."

Sophie was already at the back door. "I'm so glad that Joshua is the handsome prince – I mean, supposing it had been someone really gross – he has to kiss me for goodness sake."

"I hardly think someone who isn't handsome would be picked to play the handsome prince," said Peter.

Kate's mum was just coming out with the washing. "I'm just hanging these sheets on the line then I'm taking Edward shopping," she told Kate. "And don't let that duck indoors," she added. "I don't want him on my carpet."

"He'll be all right, Mum," said Kate.

"He won't be any trouble."

Sophie put the video in the machine and Kate looked over to the French windows. Quackers was just outside, watching her, with his head on one side. He looked puzzled.

"I won't be long," called Kate.

Quackers tapped on the glass with his beak.

"Oh, he wants to come in with me," chuckled Kate.

"Well, he can't. You know what your mum said," Sophie told her. "Now come on. It's starting." She arranged her skirt neatly round her on the chair and daintily crossed her feet.

Kate smiled over at Quackers and then sat down on the floor with Peter to watch the film. The little duck eventually disappeared from the French windows and she only saw him again once when he streaked past, little neck and beak stretched out, chasing Morgan.

They all enjoyed the film. It had just finished, and Sophie was whirling round saying how wonderful it was when they heard the scream from the garden.

"My sheets. Look what he's done to my sheets."

They ran outside to see Kate's mum had come back. She was holding up one of the sheets on the line.

"What's the matter?" cried Kate. "Who's done what?"

Quackers immediately ran to Kate and nestled up against her left foot. "That duck, that's who," said Mum. "And what he's done is pecked all along the edge of the clean sheets I had hanging on the line."

Quackers looked innocently up at Kate then nibbled gently on her shoelaces.

Kate looked at the dirty beak marks all along the bottom of the sheets.

"Yuck!" said Sophie.

"Naughty duck," said Edward.

Kate picked Quackers up and he reached up to gently nibble her chin. "I'm sorry, Mum. He's only a baby, he doesn't understand. And they were hanging very low."

"I'll have to wash them all over again," her mother grumbled, pulling the sheets off the line. "Just when I wanted to get out here and start on the weeding." She marched off muttering. "I knew he'd be trouble."

Chapter 4

Splash!

After lunch Kate went out into the garden to start the weeding. Quackers ran after her. "I've got to make it up to Mum," she told him. "I don't want her being cross with you."

The little duck stood alongside her as she loosened the soil with her trowel. "And you're going to have to learn that you can't come into the house. It's no good you sitting on the step tapping on the French windows all through lunch like you did just now. I wish I could let you in. But Mum won't allow it."

Quackers looked up at her and then down to where she was digging. Suddenly he dived forward and ate a beetle she had uncovered. He watched eagerly after that, his lightning beak retrieving roots, ants, worms, more beetles and anything else that had the misfortune to pass his beak.

Kate was enjoying herself. "I had no idea weeding could be so much fun." Quackers gave a little wag of his tiny tail and looked up at her. He looked quite comical with his beak covered in earth.

Her mother came out with the clean sheets to put them on the line again. "I must say you're making a good job of the weeding," she said.

"Quackers is helping," Kate told her. "You know all those creepy crawlies you don't like? Well, Quackers is getting rid of them for you."

"Yes, well, make sure you keep him off my sheets." She had just turned to peg a T-shirt on the line when Quackers decided to help. He rushed forward to retrieve a pair of Kate's dad's underpants that were hanging out of the washing basket. Before Kate could stop him he ran across the garden with them.

Kate gave chase and caught him when he tripped over them. She quickly separated the squirming heap of duck and underpants.

"Uh-oh. Mud." The underpants were covered in earth from his beak! Kate hid them behind her back until her mother had gone inside. Then she sneaked into the bathroom to rinse them out and put them on the line with the other washing.

"Phew," she said to Quackers. "We got away with that one, but don't you dare go near those sheets."

Quackers had a busy first week exploring his new home. He chased Morgan out of the garden several times. He ate all the dead flies out of the cobwebs (and a couple of spiders as well) and yesterday he had run after the postman, cheeping up at him. The postman had laughed and said it made a change from being chased by dogs.

Kate had found it hard leaving Quackers to go to school but she popped back at lunchtimes and he was always pleased to see her. And she had taken him into school on Friday to let the other children see how he was developing.

They had recorded that at five weeks old he weighed five hundred and three grams and that his brown-flecked wing and body feathers now covered over half of his body.

"It's Saturday again," she told Quackers, as she started cleaning out his hut. "And I'm going to spend every minute I can with you."

"Cheek-cheek."

Kate laughed. "What did you say?"

The little duck watched her with his head on one side. "Cheek-cheek."

"Oh, your little voice is changing," she chuckled. "Miss Hancock did say it would change gradually."

Peter arrived and she told him about it. He laughed. "Keep practising," he told Quackers. "You'll soon be able to quack."

"Cheek-cheek," said Quackers.

"I've been trying to get him to go into the pond," said Kate "But he's not interested. He just looks up at me all puzzled."

"Perhaps it's because he's never seen another duck," Peter suggested. "He thinks he's one of us and we don't live in water so he doesn't see why he should."

Kate chuckled. "It doesn't really matter. He's okay as long as he has a bowl of water to dip his head in. It says so in the book I got from the library."

They filled the hut with fresh straw and then went and sat on the lawn. It was unbelievably warm for the time of year.

Kate's father came and joined them. "This summer seems to be going on for ever," he said.

Quackers sat happily with them. He

was looking up and calling to the birds that flew overhead. He also called to the aeroplanes and helicopters as well.

"He's probably wondering why they don't answer him," laughed Kate.

"I can't believe how fast his feathers are growing," said Peter. "He looks just like a small female duck now."

"I'm sure he's a boy," said Kate. "I've just got this feeling – but like Miss Hancock said, we'll just have to wait until his feathers change later in the year."

Kate's father got up. "I'd better make a start. I've got to sort out some wood to build the scenery for that pantomime your class is putting on."

Her mother came out then with Edward, carrying a washing basket full of sheets.

Uh-oh, thought Kate, remembering last week's sheets on the line. "I think I'll come and help you, Dad. And bring Quackers with me. You coming, Peter?"

Peter nodded and jumped up.

"Good idea," said Mum.

"Naughty duck," said Edward.

Quackers happily followed Kate round to the big shed in the school grounds.

* * *

The next day was just as warm and Kate's mum decided to get Edward's paddling pool out for him. "I can't believe it's the beginning of October," she said. "I've never known a year like it."

Kate lay on the grass in her swimsuit with Quackers gently nibbling at her hair. It was peaceful – and there was no washing out, so no mischief for Quackers to get up to. The only sound was Edward's happy shrieks as he played in his paddling pool.

Mum got up. "I think I'll bring the lunch out here. Make the most of this glorious weather. Will you watch Edward for me, Kate?"

Kate stood up. Edward's paddling pool looked fun. "Move over, Edward," she said. "I'm getting in too while I look after you."

"Naughty Kate," said Edward, but he chuckled as she got in with him, and splashed her.

Kate laughed too and splashed him gently back.

Quackers waddled over and cocked his head on one side watching them.

"Cheek-cheek." Then with a sudden flap of his tiny wings he jumped in too. He landed between Kate and Edward with a splash.

Kate laughed. But Edward screamed and scrambled out.

Quackers swam around dipping his head in and out of the water. He was having a lovely time.

"You're swimming!" Kate cried. "Well done, Quackers."

But Edward's screams brought Mum out. She was furious. "Get out of there," she shouted at Quackers. She clapped her hands at him.

Startled, Quackers jumped out on to the side of the inflatable pool.

Kate heard the hiss as the little duck's claws punctured the material.

Chapter 5

That Duck's Got to Go

Kate jumped out and picked up Quackers just as her father arrived.

"What's going on?" Dad looked at the shrivelling paddling-pool spilling its water on to the grass, and then at Kate and Quackers. "Oh dear, what have you been up to now, young fellow-me-lad?"

Edward wailed in the background.

"Naughty duck, naughty duck, naughty duck."

"That duck's got to go," said Kate's mother. "First thing on Monday morning you're to ask Miss Hancock to take him to her rescue centre."

"No," cried Kate, hugging Quackers to her. "He didn't mean any harm. He was just enjoying himself. He was excited. It was his first time in water. He swam for the first time!"

Quackers looked up at her and she kissed him on the head. She turned to plead with her father. "He wouldn't have hurt Edward. And he only punctured the paddling pool because Mum frightened him."

"Maybe, but he's likely to do it again," said her mother. "He's a nuisance. We can't leave the back door open or he's in the house. He was in nearly every day last week when you were at school."

"He was probably looking for me," cried Kate. "He misses me."

"He frightened the life out of Grandma when she was here last week by pecking her bottom when she bent down to pick up her glasses. And on Wednesday I found beak marks on my white nightdress that was on the line."

"But, Mum, I'll pay for a new paddling pool…"

"You can't possibly afford one."

"Look, I can probably fix the paddling pool with a puncture repair outfit," said her father. "And the weather's bound to change any day now so we won't be able to use it any more this year anyway." He put his arm round his wife. "Quackers is already five weeks old, he'll be able to fly in about three weeks and will probably leave us then anyway."

"Oh, Dad," said Kate. A tear plopped on to Quackers's back and the little duck ruffled his feathers and shook himself.

"Surely we can manage till then," he continued. "If we discuss things – like putting your washing out – we can arrange a time when either Kate or I can be there to watch him. And he'll soon learn he can't come in the house."

"Please, Mum," said Kate.

"Cheek-cheek," said Quackers.

"Well…" said Mum. "I suppose so." She went back indoors to finish getting the lunch.

"And now that Quackers has been in the paddling pool, how about trying him in the pond again?" said Dad. "It'll be the first step towards his independence."

Kate nodded. She didn't want to think about him being independent and about him leaving her. But he had loved being in the paddling pool and it was natural for a duck.

She carefully carried the little duck over to the pond and put him down beside it.

Quackers looked at the water, then he looked at Kate.

"Go on then," said Kate. "In you go. Just like in the paddling pool."

He looked back at the water, then at Kate, with his head on one side. "Cheek-cheek."

Dad laughed. "I don't think he wants to go in without you."

Kate bent down and put her hand in the water. "It's freezing."

"Ducklings usually follow their mother into the water and he thinks you're his mother. That's why he followed you into the paddling pool."

"Oh dear," said Kate. Quackers was still looking up at her. He was expecting her to do something. "Oh well, here goes." She gingerly stepped into the clear water. "Ahh," she cried, as it rippled over her ankles. "Come on, Quackers. But take note, I might still have my swimming costume on but I'm not sitting in this water."

Quackers immediately plunged in after her, his little webbed feet paddling him round and round.

"There, he just needed you to show him it was okay," said Dad. "I think you've got a very special relationship with that little duck."

Kate smiled. She got out and sat on the grass watching Quackers. The excited little duck dipped and dived and paddled and floated – he was having a lovely time.

Kate helped her father again in the afternoon. It was the least she could do as he had, once again, persuaded Mum to let Quackers stay. Also she wanted to keep the little duck away from Mum as much as possible.

Lunch in the garden had been a disaster. It was bad enough Quackers adding the odd slice of bread and butter and a couple of lettuce leaves to his diet

– his lightning beak too quick for them to catch him. But when he had tried to jump up on the tray on Kate's mum's lap and tipped up her entire lunch – that had been the last straw. Everything had been packed up and taken indoors.

So Kate (and Quackers) were helping Dad to paint the scenery for the dwarfs' cottage. It was just as well they were in the big shed and not the school hall, as the headmistress would not have been impressed with the little bright-red webbed footprints all over the floor.

Quackers had jumped up on an open paint tin and upset it. Luckily it was only emulsion and they were able to wash it off him.

After that they kept the open paint tins well out of the little duck's reach.

Sophie arrived bubbling with excitement. "Guess what? I had an extra lesson with Marcus this morning."

"I know," said Kate. "You told us enough times beforehand."

"Cheek-cheek." Quackers nestled against Kate's foot, looking up at Sophie.

Sophie ignored him. "Yes, but that's not it. It's that Marcus is involved in some local workshops called Stars of Tomorrow. They're for talented young actors and he thinks I might have a chance."

"D'you want to join then?" asked Kate.

"Ooh, yes," Sophie clasped her hands together, her eyes shining. "I really do want to be an actress."

Quackers waddled forward to nibble the edge of Sophie's skirt and she pulled it away from him. "When's he going to fly away?"

Kate wished people wouldn't keep talking about him flying away. She hoped he'd stay for ever.

Chapter 6

Half-Term

By the end of October, Quackers was seven weeks old and had all his feathers. The beginnings of a white ring developing round his neck showed Kate that he probably was a male.

"I always thought you were a boy," she told him on Friday evening. "You're such a handsome little duck."

"Chack-chack," said Quackers.

Kate laughed. "You're almost there. It's 'quack'. Say 'quack'."

"Chack-chack." Quackers scratched his neck with his foot.

Kate picked him up and carried him over to his hut. "It's bedtime now but we've got the whole of next week together. It's half-term so there's no school – and no visits for you either." She usually took Quackers into school once a week for the other children to record his development on their chart.

"And there's no rehearsals for the pantomime either."

Quackers bobbed his head as he listened to her. "Chack-chack."

"It's coming on very well – the pantomime. I think we're going to raise lots of money for your friends at the Wildfowl Rescue Centre."

Quackers settled down on his straw. "And I'll tell you something else. I don't really mind being one of the seven dwarfs now. It's quite good fun. Though Marcus is a bit of a pain. He's always getting upset about something and waving his arms in the air and shouting. And he keeps calling everyone 'darling'." She went to shut the door. "Night, night, Quackers."

There was a muffled "Chack-chack" from behind the door.

* * *

It was the best half-term that Kate could ever remember. She was up early every day to go out to Quackers. It was getting colder now but she just wrapped up warmly and stayed outside with him all day.

Sometimes she would sit by the pond watching Quackers bobbing about looking for good things to eat. He was quite good at searching the bottom now.

Down would go his little head and up went his tail as his little beak sifted through the mud at the bottom.

She sometimes took a sandwich out – and shared it with him when her mother wasn't looking. Quackers's favourite was tuna fish sandwiches. And he also liked prawn cocktail crisps.

They spent quite a bit of time helping Kate's father. They'd taken all the scenery for the pantomime over to the hall and set it up. Quackers never seemed to mind what he did as long as he was with Kate.

The little duck stretched up and flapped his wings, showing the blue and white feathers underneath.

"You really are growing up fast," said Kate.

Peter arrived just as Morgan appeared over the fence. The tabby cat rarely came into the garden these days.

Quackers spotted him and took off, running across the garden. He flapped his wings as he ran and then gave a little jump in the air. Kate gasped as he landed on his beak in a heap on the lawn.

"He's trying to fly," she cried, running over to him.

Quackers scrabbled to his feet and shook himself. "Chack-chack."

"Wow," said Peter.

"Oh you clever little duck," said Kate. She was so excited, but then a heavy, sad feeling came over her. "He could be flying away soon," she said to Peter.

"Perhaps he won't," said Peter. "He obviously likes it here, don't you, Quackers?"

Quackers looked up at them and shook the grass off his beak.

Mum came out to plant some bulbs. Quackers rushed over to her. He stood alongside her, diving in with his beak to retrieve the worms and other creepy crawlies.

"Naughty duck," said Edward, who was watching.

Mum laughed. "No he's not, Edward. He's helping me."

Kate was amazed. Was Quackers winning her over?

Sophie arrived, bubbling with excitement. "I had an extra dancing lesson this morning." Her feet tapped out a quick time-step. "And guess what? My dance teacher is coming to see me in the pantomime. She's such a darling."

Peter pulled a face at Kate. Sophie had taken to copying Marcus quite a lot lately.

"Watch this." Sophie put her tongue out and moved it up and down. Then she started rolling the tip around.

"What on earth are you doing?" asked Peter.

Quackers looked up from the flowerbed but then went back to his digging.

"I'm warming up my tongue muscles, darling," said Sophie. "Marcus taught me yesterday. I had an extra session with him to go over my songs."

Kate and Peter just looked at each other. Sophie talked endlessly about Marcus these days. "Do you know why he's called Marcus Monday? Well, he told me it's because it was a Monday when he decided to become an actor. And did you know that he's very superstitious?"

"We could hardly miss that," said Kate. "He told me off for bringing an open umbrella indoors last week."

"Lots of actors are superstitious," said Sophie. She backed off as Quackers ran towards them, his beak covered in earth. "Have you seen the stone that Marcus wears round his neck?"

"Can't miss it," said Peter. "It swings about when he's getting agitated."

"Yes, well that's his lucky stone – a talisman it's called."

Kate guessed what she was going to say next. And she was right.

"I thought I might get myself a

talisman to bring me luck," said Sophie.
She looked down at Quackers again and
spotted the worm hanging out of his
beak. "Yuck! That's disgusting."

They heard a lorry pull up out the front. Quackers hastily threw his head back and swallowed his worm. Then he ran towards the lorry, flapping his wings and making little jumps every now and then. "Chack-chack. Chack-chack."

They all followed Quackers round to the front of the house. "Oh look, darlings," cried Sophie. "It's a red lorry. That reminds me of a tongue twister

Marcus taught me: Red lorry, yellow lorry. You have to keep saying it as fast as you can without getting muddled up."

Peter rolled his eyes to the top of his head and Kate chuckled. There was no stopping Sophie.

On the back of the lorry was a huge fish tank and Kate's father came out to help the driver unload it.

"I've borrowed it from a friend of mine at the zoo," he explained. "It's to be the glass case that Snow White is put in after she's eaten the poisoned apple."

"You mean I've got to lie in a fish tank?" cried Sophie.

"It hasn't been used," said Kate's dad. "And I'm sure Marcus thinks you're a good enough actress to make it look convincing."

Sophie agreed but still had a funny look on her face.

The tank was actually made of Perspex so it wasn't too heavy. They all helped carry it round to the school hall.

Quackers liked the look of the tank. He waddled round the outside of it occasionally rapping his beak on it. Then, with a sudden flap of his wings and a big jump, he landed inside it.

"Wow," said Peter.

"He'll be flying properly soon," said Dad.

"I know," said Kate, sadly.

Quackers waddled round and round in the tank making quiet little 'chacking' noises to himself.

"I think it reminds him of the tank he was born in," said Kate.

"Probably," Peter chuckled. "Anyway I'd better go home for tea now."

"So had I, darling," said Sophie. "I'll come with you."

As Peter passed Kate he whispered to her: "If she calls me 'darling' one more time I'll scream."

Kate watched them as they walked out of the gate and up the road. Then she heard Peter scream.

Chapter 7

Rehearsals

Kate let Quackers out of his hut and gave him his breakfast. "I've got to go back to school today," she told him. "But I'll come and see you at lunchtime."

The little duck watched as she went out of the gate.

Kate had just gone into the playground when she heard it. A flapping sound

behind her. She turned to see Quackers
flying over the fence after her.

"Quackers!" Kate watched open-
mouthed as the little duck flew down
towards her. With legs outstretched and
wings held back he landed in the
playground and pitched right over,
landing in a heap of squeaks and
feathers.

"Oh, Quackers," cried Kate, rushing to him. "Are you all right?"

The little duck got up and shook himself. "Quack-quack," he said proudly. "Quack-quack, quack-quack, quack-quack."

"You can quack. And you can fly. All in the same day. You clever little duck. And you're only just eight weeks old."

Tears rolled down Kate's cheeks. She was excited and sad at the same time. "You're so grown up now. But please don't leave me. Not yet."

The rest of the class were excited too and Miss Hancock had difficulty getting them to concentrate on their lessons. From the window they could see Quackers waddling around in the playground.

Kate spent an anxious morning wondering if he would still be there when they went outside for break and then for lunchtime. He was – he ran to greet Kate as soon as she came out of the door.

After lunch it was time for the pantomime rehearsal. Kate followed the other children across the playground to the school hall. Quackers followed Kate, quacking excitedly.

"He's been used to being in the hall with me during the holidays," Kate told Miss Hancock. "We've been helping Dad with the scenery."

"Yes, well I don't think Marcus will be too happy to see him," said Miss Hancock. "I think he'd better wait outside."

So Quackers was left sitting on the step. He watched forlornly through the glass door. Kate kept looking over to him and waving – when Marcus wasn't looking. She could see his little beak opening and shutting as he called to her.

Then it was her turn to be on stage with the other six dwarfs to rehearse their song. Marcus was waving his long thin arms about and shouting: "I want you to make it real. Make it live."

Kate rolled her eyes. He did get carried away.

Marcus rushed to the piano and played the introduction.

The seven dwarfs started: "Hi ho, hi ho, it's off to work we go…"

Marcus was instantly on his feet again, his unruly hair flopping over his eyes. "More volume," he shouted. "They can't hear you at the back."

The next attempt was better and Marcus wanted them to sing it while marching across the stage. He ran his hands through his tangled hair and went back to the piano. "It's stuffy in here," he said. "Can someone open the door?"

The music started.

Someone opened the door.

Quackers shot in.

The seven dwarfs started marching across the stage.

Quackers raced down to the front, flapping his wings and flew up onto the stage. Before anyone could stop him he had joined in on the end of the line of dwarfs, waddling along behind Kate.

Everyone burst out laughing.

The music stopped. Marcus wasn't laughing. He leapt to his feet waving his arms about. "This is too much. *Too* much. Put him out someone."

But Quackers was too quick for them. He jumped off the stage and hid underneath it. No one could get at him there so they had to continue.

Sophie was on stage when he decided to make his second entrance. She was singing "Some Day My Prince Will Come" when Quackers appeared on the stage behind her.

"Quack-quack, quack-quack."

"Here he is, Sophie," shouted Adrian. "Your Prince is here."

Everyone laughed but Sophie and Marcus were furious. Kate quickly caught him before he could disappear again and put him outside. The door was shut again.

Quackers began rapping on the door with his beak. He ran up and down quacking so loudly that they could hear him through the closed door.

"This is too much. *Too* much," cried Marcus. "I can't concentrate with that row going on."

Then Quackers disappeared for a moment and re-appeared as he crashed into the closed window trying to fly through it.

"Oh no!" Kate rushed outside. Several of the other children and Miss Hancock followed.

"Quackers! Are you hurt?" Kate had

tears in her eyes as she gently picked him up. She anxiously looked him over. He was dazed but fortunately not injured. "Oh, thank goodness," she breathed. She turned to Miss Hancock. "He could have really hurt himself."

"I know, dear," said the teacher. "Although I don't think he'll do it again. But I'll have a word with Marcus."

Marcus was tearing at his hair. "Come back, everyone. This is madness. How can we put on a pantomime with a crazy duck and half the cast leaving every five minutes?"

Miss Hancock went over to talk to him. Kate couldn't hear all that was said but she heard bits like "flying away any day now" and "less disruption if we let him stay". Marcus did a lot of arm waving.

Then Marcus addressed the class. "Okay – we're going to try letting him stay. But you –" he pointed a long thin finger at Kate – "keep an eye on him."

Quackers made a feeble attempt to bite the finger but Marcus was too quick pulling it away.

Kate was actually relieved to see Quackers try that. He couldn't be feeling too bad. She sat down with the little duck on her lap and gently stroked his feathers. "You must be careful of windows," she whispered to him. "I couldn't bear it if you were hurt."

The little duck sat quietly on Kate's lap through the next couple of scenes. Then they went on to the scene where the wicked queen is talking to her magic mirror. Cathy and Peter were on stage.

Quackers suddenly jumped off Kate's lap. He was obviously feeling better. Kate wasn't quick enough to stop him, but all eyes were on the wicked queen as he slipped under the stage. Kate decided to leave him there until after the scene – Marcus didn't like interruptions and he was already in a bad mood. Apart from

Quackers upsetting him, Emma had taken her shoes off to dance and had put them on a table.

"Don't you know it's unlucky to put shoes on the table?" he had shouted at her.

Now Marcus was waving his long thin arms about again and shouting to Peter who was standing behind the mirror. "As soon as the wicked queen has finished speaking, pull the curtain on the mirror across to reveal yourself. Then make your speech."

"Okay," came Peter's voice from behind the curtain.

Cathy (the wicked queen) began: "Mirror, mirror on the wall, who is the fairest of them all?"

Silence.

Marcus ran his fingers through his

tangled hair. "Come on. Pick up your cue. What are you waiting for?"

Cathy began again. "Mirror, mirror on the wall, who is the fairest of them all?"

Peter drew the curtain across to reveal himself – and Quackers who was sitting happily on his feet.

"Quack-quack, quack-quack."

"Oh no," shouted Marcus, shaking his head and making his hair flop about all over the place. "This is too much. *Too much.*"

Quackers retreated under the stage and they went on to the scene in the palace kitchens. Sophie, as Snow White, was with Marcus as Clara the pantomime dame. Clara was supposed to be making a cake and making a complete mess of it.

It was very funny. Kate couldn't help laughing. But then Quackers popped out again. He looked up at the stage and the table with the cloth on it. It reminded him of the low hanging sheets on the washing line that he liked to peck. He flew up on to the stage and pulled at the cloth. It came off dragging everything else with it.

Marcus turned bright red with rage. Everyone else (except Sophie) tried hard not to laugh

"It is supposed to be a funny scene," Peter pointed out.

"Yes, but *I'm* supposed to be funny," said Marcus. "Not the duck."

After that, apart from jumping up at the wicked queen for a share of the poisoned apple, Quackers seemed to calm down. He just wandered about quacking gently to himself.

That is until Sophie was lying in the glass case with her arms folded over her chest.

Marcus was trying to persuade the handsome prince to kiss her. "You don't have to like her," he was saying, running his hands through his tangled mass of hair. "It's acting. Sophie probably doesn't want you to kiss her either but at least she's acting like a professional."

Kate saw Sophie's lips twitch – she was trying not to smile – after all she was supposed to be unconscious.

Quackers stretched his neck and eyed the scene. He liked the glass case. And he liked Sophie. He decided to join her.

Sophie screamed as the excited duck, quacking loudly, landed on top of her.

She was almost hysterical as she scrambled out. "I can't do this. I can't do this," she cried. "How can anyone act properly with that – that creature in here?"

Quackers waddled around in the glass case quacking gently to himself, quite unaware of the chaos he had caused.

Marcus rushed over to comfort Sophie. "This is too much. *Too* much," she sobbed, mimicking his expression.

Marcus pulled a chunk of hair out and waved the other hand in the air. "I can't put up with any more. If that duck is still here next week you're going to have to keep him out!"

Chapter 8

Seven is a Special Number

Quackers was still there the next week. Kate was delighted. The little duck often flew over the garden or over the playground now. Every time he took off Kate watched, holding her breath, hoping desperately that he wouldn't fly away. But so far he had returned to her every time.

Keeping him out of the pantomime rehearsal was easier said than done. He got in when Joshua went out to go to the toilet. And then again when he came back. Then he slipped under the stage where no one could get him.

Another week passed with Kate watching and worrying every time Quackers took off. But he still hadn't flown away. At the next rehearsal he slipped in when the headmistress came to see how they were getting on.

Every time he got in, Marcus appeared to tear out another handful of hair. Kate thought it was a good job he had plenty or he would be bald by now.

As yet another week went by Kate couldn't believe that Quackers was still with her. His head was beginning to turn green and silver-grey feathers were growing on his body and wings. He was nearly fully-grown.

"He doesn't seem to want to leave us, does he?" Kate's mother said to her. Quackers had definitely won her over. He came waddling up to get the sardine she had for him. She often saved special titbits for him now. "He's been helping me in the garden again. And he hasn't tried to come in the house lately."

"I think he's grown out of that. He seems to like spending time in the pond or over at the school," said Kate. "Don't you?" she said to Quackers.

The little duck looked up. "Quack-quack."

"Doesn't Miss Hancock mind him being at the school?"

"No, she loves him. Anyway he doesn't come into the classroom much. It's just the pantomime rehearsals he insists on coming into."

Actually he hadn't been too badly behaved at the last rehearsal. (He'd got in when Marcus himself had gone out to speak to Kate's dad about the scenery.) He'd seemed content to wander amongst the children quacking gently to himself. The one thing they could never stop him doing though, was joining in on the end of the line of dwarfs. He loved waddling along behind Kate.

Kate sat down with Quackers when her mother went indoors. "I'm so glad you haven't flown away yet," she told him. "Perhaps you'll stay – at least until Christmas."

"Quack-quack, quack-quack." The little duck expertly used his yellow bill to preen his feathers carefully.

The pantomime was only two weeks away now and all the tickets had been sold. Decorations had been put up in the hall, and a large Christmas tree. Quackers liked to nibble the bottom branches and he constantly watched the decorations with his head on one side.

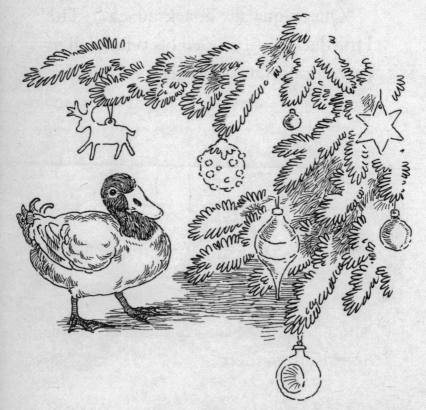

Everyone was excited. Especially Sophie as Marcus had arranged for his friends from the Stars of Tomorrow Workshops to come and watch her.

Then disaster struck. There was a flu epidemic!

One by one the cast went down with it. Kate and Peter caught it early on so were back before the performance. Sophie was beside herself with worry and kept well away from everyone. But she still caught it, with only a few days to go before the show.

"She'll never be better in time," Kate said to Quackers. "Everyone else has been off for a week with it."

The dress rehearsal was held on the afternoon before the performance. It was the last day of term.

Quackers followed Kate over to the hall. He was now a very handsome drake with a glossy green head, a white collar round his throat, a brown breast and silver-grey body and wings. His stiff tail feathers curved smartly upwards.

Kate's father joked that he'd got a new coat for Christmas.

Although Quackers flew quite regularly now he showed no signs of wanting to leave Kate. He was still very attached to her. But Kate still worried, she knew he could go at any time.

Sophie turned up – just in time for the rehearsal. She was still clearly unwell.

"You look terrible," said Kate. "You should have stayed in bed."

"I had to come, darling," she said, her voice trembling. "The show must go on."

"I know Snow White is supposed to

have a pale skin," whispered Adrian, looking at her. "But that's over the top."

"She isn't supposed to have a red nose though," said Emma.

Quackers watched from under the stage as they all changed into their costumes. (He had slipped in when Miss Hancock went out to get some safety pins.)

Marcus called everyone together. There was still a lot of the cast away.

"I'm going to juggle you around to see if there's enough of you to cover all the main parts," he told them. "Luckily Sophie has managed to come in. We certainly couldn't do it without Snow White."

Sophie managed a half smile at that.

Marcus started to sort the cast out. Some of them could double up to play another part as well as their own.

He cut the number of villagers right down and Miss Hancock and Kate's father said they could do the scene shifting.

Quackers stayed under the stage. It was almost as though he realized he shouldn't interrupt today.

Marcus looked at the depleted cast

and ran his long fingers through his tangled hair. He looked at his notes. Then back at the children.

"It's no good," he said. "I've cut the parts down as much as I can but we're still one dwarf short."

"We'll just have to have six dwarfs instead of seven then," said Peter.

"Impossible," cried Marcus, throwing his arms in the air. "We must have seven dwarfs."

Miss Hancock shook her head. "I don't think anyone else is likely to be back by this evening. I've phoned the parents of the children still off and they're all still pretty bad."

"That's it then," said Marcus. "We'll have to cancel."

Sophie looked as though she was going to faint. The dark circles under her eyes got even darker. Kate rushed to help support her.

"Perhaps we could do it after Christmas," said Miss Hancock.

Marcus shook his head. "I've just got a part in a play up North. I leave to start rehearsals the day after Boxing Day. The play should run well into the summer and by then everyone will have forgotten their parts. And anyway you can't have a pantomime in the summer."

He threw his long arms up in the air. "It's no good."

Sophie straightened up and glared at Marcus. Her face was very pale and drawn. "We can't cancel. Not after all this work. And I've got out of bed to come here. Why can't we do it with only six dwarfs? Most people probably won't even notice."

The rest of the cast joined in with her in agreement.

"No." Marcus held up his hand to silence them. "I'm just as upset as you are by this decision but it'll be unlucky to go on with only six dwarfs. There must be seven. Snow White has never been performed with less. Seven is a special, even magical, number."

Chapter 9

A Quacking Good Performance

Sophie burst into tears and sobbed uncontrollably. Kate felt sorry for her. She had really worked hard for this. It had been her big chance. Why did stupid Marcus have to be so superstitious?

"We'll have to give everyone their money back," said Miss Hancock.

"But we were going to give it all to the Wildfowl Rescue Centre," cried Kate.

"I'll tell my friends from the workshops not to come," said Marcus.

Sophie let out a howl.

Quackers popped out and looked up at Sophie. Kate chewed thoughtfully on her pigtail as she looked at him. She thought of how many more little creatures like him could have been helped with the money from the pantomime.

The idea came to her so suddenly that she felt as though she had been slapped in the face. "That's it," she shouted.

Everyone turned to look at her.

She was quivering with excitement. "Here you are, Marcus," she cried, pointing to Quackers. "Here's your seventh dwarf."

"Don't be ridiculous," said Marcus.

Sophie immediately stopped howling

and looked up. "It's not ridiculous," she said. "He knows what to do. He's done it often enough."

Peter joined in. "Surely there's nothing unlucky about having a duck on stage, is there?"

"Well, I've never heard anything—"

"He's lucky, don't you see," cried Sophie. "He can save the pantomime. Please, Marcus. *Please*." She stamped her foot.

Marcus rubbed his stubbly chin. "Well I suppose as long as there are seven it shouldn't matter if one is a duck." He broke into a huge grin. "Okay. Let's give it a go."

Everyone cheered.

"Quack-quack, quack-quack, quack-quack," said Quackers, running round everyone's feet.

Marcus started laughing and Kate wondered if perhaps he'd actually forgiven Quackers for biting his nose.

* * *

Quackers had a wonderful time. Kate's mum had made him a tiny green cloak, which matched his glossy green head perfectly.

Marcus said he was the best duck actor he had ever met, as Quackers proudly marched along after Kate. The Seven Dwarfs' song was a bit unusual: "Hi ho, quack, hi ho, quack, it's off to work we go, quack." The audience roared.

He only appeared on stage a couple of times when he wasn't supposed to. Once when the villagers were dancing, but the children just danced round him while he quacked in the middle. Then again when Marcus was on stage on his own in the castle kitchen. Marcus had on a huge, wide purple dress with long yellow and black stripped stockings. And he wore a bright orange wig which looked very funny. Although Kate did wonder why he bothered with a wig – his own hair looked pretty funny. The audience spotted Quackers and shouted to Marcus: "He's behind you."

Marcus quickly entered into the spirit of it and instantly replied: "Oh no he isn't."

The audience roared back: "Oh yes he is."

In the interval Marcus told Sophie that his friends were so impressed with her already that they were going to offer her a place in the Stars of Tomorrow workshops. He was in such a good mood that he even joked to Kate about Quackers being offered a place.

Kate, Peter and Quackers watched Sophie from the wings during the second half. "She is good," whispered Kate. "And she's not at all well."

"Who knows, perhaps one day she'll be famous," whispered Peter. "And we'll be boasting that we were in her first production."

"Quack-quack," said Quackers.

"You've been such a good boy," said Kate. "But I think I'd better hang on to you when Sophie is in the glass case, just in case you can't resist joining her."

The final scene was the wedding when Snow White married the handsome prince. Sophie had on a lovely white wedding dress with a long flowing train.

The seven dwarfs were to carry her train and Quackers proudly took his place amongst them holding on to it with his beak.

"He probably thinks it's a sheet," whispered Kate.

At the end they all came forward to take their bows. The audience clapped loudly.

Sophie's pale face was now flushed and she had tears streaming down it. She bent down to Quackers and pushed him gently forward to take a special bow on his own.

The audience went wild, clapping and cheering, completely drowning out his excited quacks.

The following day the local paper reported that the pantomime had raised a lot of money for the Wildfowl Rescue Centre and had been a huge success. Snow White's nose had been a bit red and the seventh dwarf was a duck – but it all contributed to making it one of the most imaginative pantomimes the reporter had ever seen. He thought it was a brilliant idea to have a duck starring in a pantomime that was to raise money for a wildfowl organization.

He predicted that Sophie had a great future as an actress but that Quackers had been the undoubted star of the show. Kate thought that even Sophie wouldn't mind being upstaged by a duck on this occasion.

Kate showed the picture in the paper to Quackers. "Look, you're famous."

Quackers nibbled the edge of the newspaper.

Kate laughed. "Oh, I hope you stay for ever. But at least if you do fly away I'll have this to remember you by. And perhaps you'll come back again. Maybe even bring a wife and baby ducklings to see me."

She gently kissed the top of his glossy head. "Happy Christmas, Quackers."

The End